Good little

WOLF

Nadia Shireen

ALFRED A. KNOPF ❧ NEW YORK

Are we all sitting
comfortably?
Then let's begin . . .

Rolf and Mrs. Boggins were best friends.
"You really are a good little wolf," Mrs. Boggins told him.
Rolf liked being a good little wolf.

He liked baking
tasty cakes.

He ate up all
his vegetables.

And he was always
nice to his friends.

But Mrs. Boggins also said that not *all* wolves were good. In fact, some were downright bad.

Rolf hoped he would never bump into a big bad wolf.

"Now, what do we have here?"
said the Big Bad Wolf.

"You LOOK like a wolf . . .

You FEEL like a wolf . . .

You SMELL like a wolf . . ."

"That's because I AM a wolf," piped up Rolf.
"I'm a very good little wolf."

"Good?" said the Big Bad Wolf.
"Wolves aren't good!
Wolves are BIG and BAD."

"Real wolves howl at the moon!"
hooted the Big Bad Wolf.
"Real wolves blow houses in!
Real wolves eat people up!"

"Well," said Rolf. "I am a real wolf.
And I'm sure I can do all of
those things."

So Rolf tried to howl at the moon.

He pursed his lips, took a deep breath,
and out came a great big . . . whistle.

Then Rolf went to see Little Pig.

"Do you mind if I blow your house in?" asked Rolf.

"You can try, I suppose," said Little Pig.

So he huffed . . .

And he puffed . . .

But it was no use.

"I'm sorry, Rolf,"
said Little Pig.

"You're right!" said Rolf sadly.
"I'm just not bad enough to be
a real wolf."

"Well . . . there is one last thing you
can do to prove you're a proper wolf,"
said the Big Bad Wolf.

And suddenly, something quite
strange came over Rolf.

He felt an unfamiliar, wild feeling
growing inside him . . .

Rolf had never felt
more like a wolf.

AROO

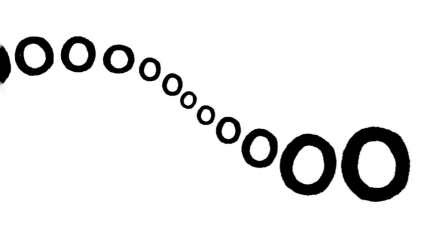

"See? I am a proper wolf.
I just happen to be a
GOOD little wolf," said Rolf.

"This calls for a celebration!" cried Mrs. Boggins.
And they all sat down for some tea and cake.

"Will you stop eating people up,
Big Bad Wolf?" asked Rolf.

"Oh, I suppose so," said the Big Bad Wolf . . .

"I'll stop first thing tomorrow."

THIS IS A BORZOI BOOK
PUBLISHED BY ALFRED A. KNOPF

Copyright © 2011 by Nadia Shireen
All rights reserved. Published in the United States by Alfred A.
Knopf, an imprint of Random House Children's Books, a division
of Random House, Inc., New York. Originally published in hardcover in
Great Britain by Jonathan Cape, an imprint of Random House Children's
Books, a division of the Random House Group Limited, London. Knopf, Borzoi
Books, and the colophon are registered trademarks of Random House, Inc.

Visit us on the Web! www.randomhouse.com/kids
Educators and librarians, for a variety of teaching tools,
visit us at www.randomhouse.com/teachers

Library of Congress Cataloging-in-Publication Data is available upon request.
ISBN 978-0-375-86904-4 (trade) — ISBN 978-0-375-96904-1 (lib. bdg.)

The illustrations in this book were created using pencil, ink,
collage, and digital rendering.

MANUFACTURED IN CHINA
September 2011
10 9 8 7 6 5 4 3 2 1
First American Edition

Random House Children's Books supports
the First Amendment and celebrates
the right to read.

For my mum and in memory of my dad. With love x

Clara Barton

by Lola M. Schaefer

Consulting Editor: Gail Saunders-Smith, Ph.D.
Consultants: The Staff of the
Clara Barton National Historical Site
Glen Echo, Maryland

Pebble Books

an imprint of Capstone Press
Mankato, Minnesota

Pebble Books are published by Capstone Press
151 Good Counsel Drive, P.O. Box 669, Mankato, Minnesota 56002
http://www.capstone-press.com

1 2 3 4 5 6 07 06 05 04 03 02

Library of Congress Cataloging-in-Publication Data
Schaefer, Lola M., 1950–
    Clara Barton / by Lola M. Schaefer.
        p. cm.—(First biographies)
    Summary: Simple text and photographs present the life of Clara Barton, who
worked as a nurse during the Civil War and founded the American Red Cross
Society in 1881 to help people hurt by war or disasters.
    Includes bibliographical references and index.
    ISBN 0-7368-1434-5 (hardcover)
    ISBN 0-7368-9410-1 (paperback)
    1. Barton, Clara, 1821–1912—Juvenile literature. 2. Red Cross—United States—
Biography—Juvenile literature. 3. Nurses—United States—Biography—Juvenile
literature. [1. Barton, Clara, 1821-1912. 2. Nurses. 3. Women—Biography.]
I. Title. II. Series.
HV569.B3 .S33 2003
361.7′634′092—dc21   2002001216

Note to Parents and Teachers

The First Biographies series supports national history standards for
units on people and culture. This book describes and illustrates the
life of Clara Barton. The photographs support early readers in
understanding the text. This book also introduces early readers to
subject-specific vocabulary words, which are defined in the Words
to Know section. Early readers may need assistance to read some
words and to use the Table of Contents, Words to Know, Read
More, Internet Sites, and Index/Word List sections of the book.

Table of Contents

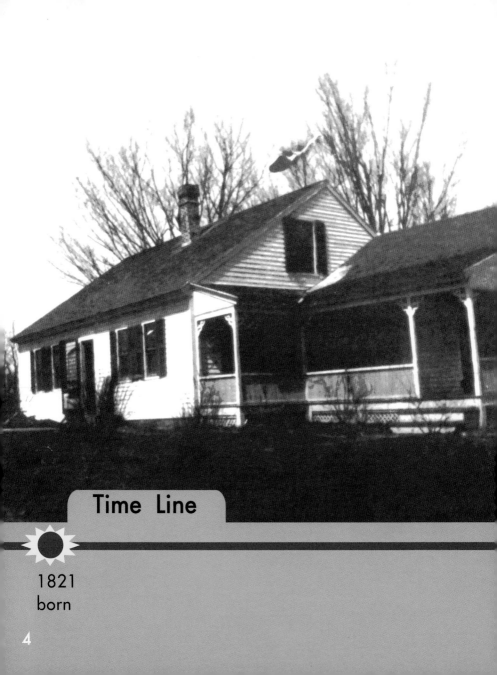

Time Line

1821
born

4

Clara Barton was born in Massachusetts in 1821. She had two older brothers and two older sisters.

 birthplace of Clara Barton in North Oxford, Massachusetts

Time Line

1821
born

1833–1835
takes care of
brother David

Clara's brother David was hurt badly in a fall. Clara took care of him for two years until he was better.

Clara's brother David grew up to be a soldier.

Time Line

```
●              ●              ☀
1821           1833–1835      1839
born           takes care of  becomes a
               brother David  teacher
```

8

Clara became a teacher. She taught in a one-room schoolhouse. She liked teaching. Clara taught for 13 years.

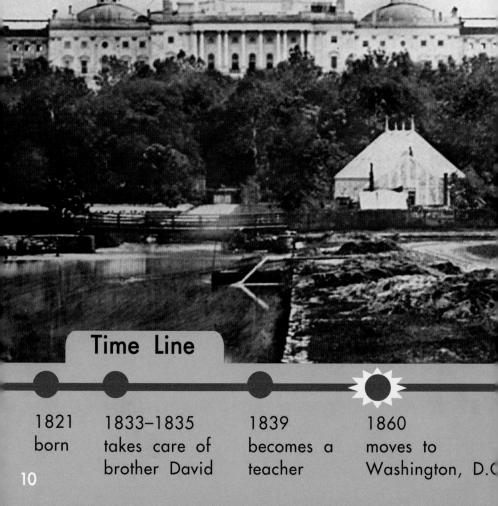

Time Line

1821
born

1833–1835
takes care of
brother David

1839
becomes a
teacher

1860
moves to
Washington, D.C

In 1860, Clara moved to Washington, D.C. Soon, the Civil War began. Clara knew that soldiers needed food, clothing, and other supplies. She wanted to help.

Washington, D.C., around 1860

1861
Civil War
begins

Time Line

1821 born	1833–1835 takes care of brother David	1839 becomes a teacher	1860 moves to Washington, D.C

Clara wrote to newspapers. She asked people to send supplies for the soldiers. Next, she asked to visit the battlefields to bring supplies to the soldiers.

W.M. Allixon

Time Line

1821 born	1833–1835 takes care of brother David	1839 becomes a teacher	1860 moves to Washington, D.C

Clara helped hurt soldiers on the battlefields. She fed them and fixed their wounds. She was kind to them. Soldiers called Clara the "Angel of the Battlefield."

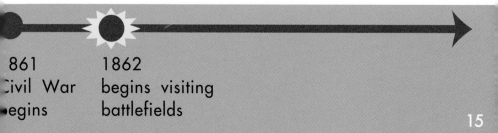

861
Civil War
begins

1862
begins visiting
battlefields

15

Time Line

1821	1833–1835	1839	1860
born	takes care of brother David	becomes a teacher	moves to Washington, D.C

After the war, many soldiers were missing. Clara helped families find about 22,000 missing or dead soldiers.

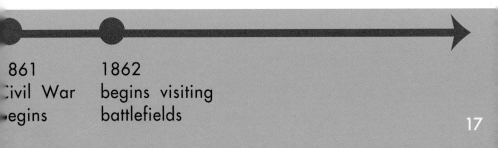

861
:ivil War
:egins

1862
begins visiting
battlefields

17

American
Red Cross

Time Line

1821	1833–1835	1839	1860
born	takes care of	becomes a	moves to
	brother David	teacher	Washington, D.C

18

In 1881, Clara created the American Red Cross Society. This group helps people hurt by war or disasters. It gives them supplies, food, and the help they need to get better.

◄ American Red Cross Society headquarters in Glen Echo, Maryland

861
ivil War
egins

1862
begins visiting
battlefields

1881
creates American
Red Cross Society

19

Time Line

| 1821 born | 1833–1835 takes care of brother David | 1839 becomes a teacher | 1860 moves to Washington, D.C |

Clara Barton died in 1912. Today, the American Red Cross still helps people hurt by war or disasters.

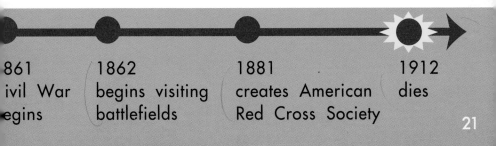

861
ivil War
egins

1862
begins visiting
battlefields

1881
creates American
Red Cross Society

1912
dies

21

Words to Know

American Red Cross Society—an organization that helps people hurt by disasters, such as floods, earthquakes, fires, or war; Clara Barton created the American Red Cross Society in 1881.

battlefield—the ground where soldiers fight

Civil War—the U.S. war between the Northern states and the Southern states; the Civil War was fought from 1861 to 1865.

disaster—an event that causes great damage, loss, or suffering; disasters include floods, tornados, fires, and wars.

soldier—someone who is in the military

supplies—materials needed to do something; Clara gathered supplies such as bandages, soap, and food for Civil War soldiers.

wound—an injury or cut

Read More

Ruffin, Francis E. *Clara Barton.* American Legends. New York: PowerKids Press, 2002.

Wheeler, Jill C. *Clara Barton.* Portraits of Inspiration. Minneapolis: Abdo Publishing, 2002.

Woodworth, Deborah. *Compassion: The Story of Clara Barton.* Plymouth, Minn.: Child's World, 1998.

Internet Sites

Clara Barton
http://www.galegroup.com/free_resources/whm/bio/barton_c.htm

Clara Barton, 1821–1912
http://www.americancivilwar.com/women/cb.html

Clara Barton National Historic Site
http://www.nps.gov/clba

Index/Word List

Word Count: 201
Early-Intervention Level: 22

Editorial Credits

Martha E. H. Rustad, editor; Heather Kindseth, series designer; Linda Clavel,
  illustrator; Patrick Dentinger, book designer; Wanda Winch, photo researcher;
  Karen Risch, product planning editor

Photo Credits

American Red Cross, 18 (inset)
Clara Barton National Historic Site, National Park Service, cover, 1, 4, 6, 8,
  16 (both), 18, 20
Corbis, 10, 12
Library of Congress/William M. Allison, 14